ABC Safari

For Richard, who would have been proud; and for Marilyn, who is–KJL
Thanks to Ron Fricke, Vice President of Education at the Philadelphia Zoo,
for verifying the accuracy of the information in this book.

Text & Illustration Copyright © 2007 Karen Lee

Publisher's Cataloging-In-Publication Data
Lee, Karen (Karen Jones), 1961-
ABC safari / [Karen Lee].
[32] p. : col. ill. ; cm.
ISBN: 978-0-9777423-0-1 (hardcover)
ISBN: 978-0-9777423-6-3 (pbk.)
1. Animals--Juvenile literature. 2. Animals.
3. Alphabet rhymes. I. Title.
QL49 .L44 2007
590   2006924848

The "For Creative Minds"
educational section may be copied
by the owner for personal use or by educators
using copies in classroom settings.

Printed in China

Sylvan Dell Publishing
976 Houston Northcutt Blvd., Suite 3
Mt. Pleasant, SC 29464

He slyly waits in log disguise.
A greedy gleam shines in his eyes.
He'll wait until the moment's right,
then **A**lligator's going to bite.

This creature loves to cut down trees–
long teeth can handle that with ease.
She stacks the logs into a dome
which then becomes the **B**eaver's home.

At quickest pace
you run your race.
But you'll be passed–
the **C**heetah's fast.

A flip, a spin, a playful leap,
she slips through waves, then dives down deep.
These joyful jumps are a jubilee
because the **D**olphin loves the sea.

Her fanciful ears fan hot air away
from crepe-paper skin that's wrinkled and gray.
Her versatile trunk's not only a nose,
when **E**lephant bathes, she makes it a hose.

The setting sun will soon inspire
the tuneless crooning of the choir.
They'll sing a chorus and rejoice
then **F**rog will add his croaking voice.

The greatest of apes, none that are bigger,
can crash through the jungle with muscle and vigor.
Although he's well known for his bone-crushing power,
the gentle **G**orilla will cradle a flower.

So big and bulky on dry land,
this heavy hulk can hardly stand.
But she can swim with buoyant grace.
The river is the **H**ippo's place.

While stretched out on a limb to rest,
light plays across his spiky crest.
Serenely lying still, it seems
Iguana's lost in daytime dreams.

Her sensitive ears catch the sneakiest sound
then gigantic feet leap away with a bound.
She zigs, then she zags to her chaser's dismay.
How swiftly the **J**ackrabbit races away!

A leafy room in tree top eaves
is just the place to dine on leaves.
Then up the branchy stairs to bed,
Koala rests his sleepy head.

A regal heart beats proud inside
the royal ruler of the pride.
You'll know him by his noble mane,
the **L**ion, king of his domain.

She floats through the bay like a whiskered, gray lump
while grazing on sea grass to keep herself plump.
Her layer of blubber and thick skin will keep
the mild mannered **M**anatee's beauty down deep.

Within the forest dark and cool,
it's hard to find his hidden pool.
Beneath the leaves he darts inside—
a secret place for Newt to hide.

The silent wings take flight
to prowl the sky at night.
Small creatures fear the scowl
of the wise and watchful Owl.

Up steep slopes she'll slip and slide,
then race downhill in headfirst glide.
This bird can soar, not through the skies–
but in the water, the **P**enguin flies.

The bobbing plume keeps perfect beat
to slow and steady pacing feet.
A speckled back keeps him concealed
as cautious **Q**uail scouts through his field.

His face is fiercely sprouting horns.
Just "keep away" his grimace warns.
But truly he's a gentle guy.
The **R**hino's really rather shy.

Performing a jump with a flippery kick,
she catches the crest in a wave-riding trick.
Returning submerged with the ebb of the tide,
the **S**ea Lion's ready to catch the next ride.

A flash of golden streaked with black,
she's poised and crouching for attack.
Beware the low and fearsome growl
of stealthy **T**iger on the prowl.

He scales rocky slopes with a hop and a skip
and climbs up a cliff to the outermost tip.
He soars to the peak with a breathtaking leap;
the **U**rial sure is a sure-footed sheep.

The highway filet is the special today.
It's all you can eat at the road-kill café.
To dine on the dead is a horrible feast,
but hard-hearted **V**ulture's not bothered the least.

This hungry hunter in the wild
is feared by woman, man, and child.
The mournful howling of the pack
is warning of the **W**olf's attack.

Her skin's so thin you look right through
to guts and bones exposed to view.
If what's inside were also clear,
the **X**-Ray Fish would disappear.

On mountain tops the wind can blow
a freezing breeze with ice and snow.
But even in the coldest storm,
the winter-coated **Y**ak stays warm.

The elegant striping of black over white
creates a refined and unusual sight.
He's more than a horse with a high fashion flair,
'cause **Z**ebras don't have to decide what to wear.

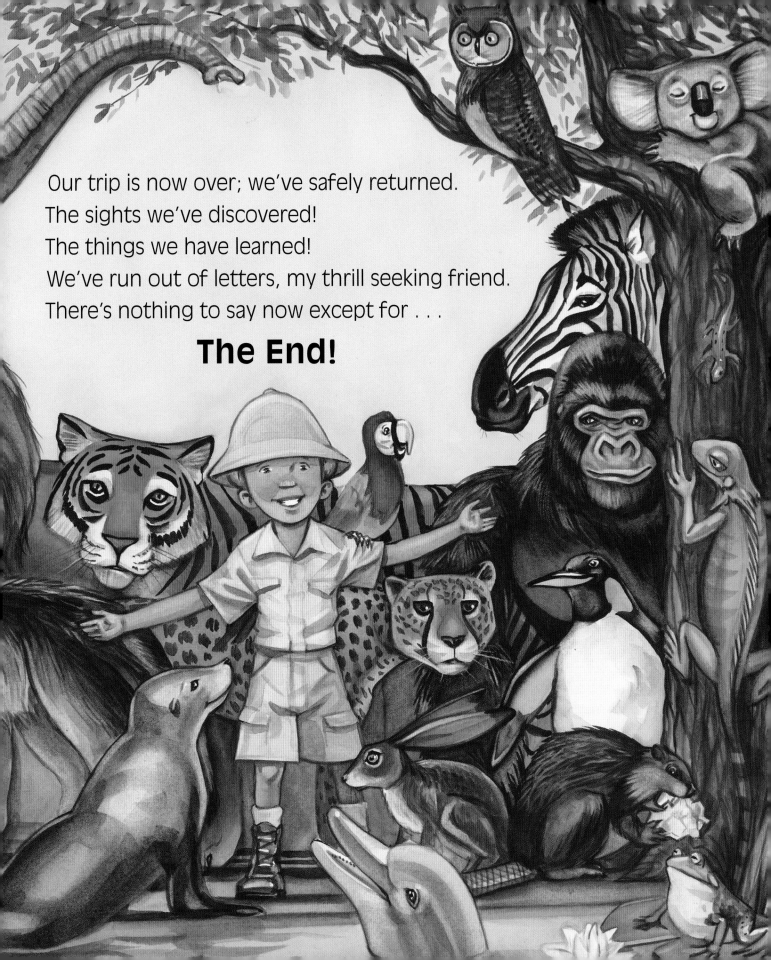

Our trip is now over; we've safely returned.
The sights we've discovered!
The things we have learned!
We've run out of letters, my thrill seeking friend.
There's nothing to say now except for . . .

The End!

For Creative Minds

Aa

Alligators

Reptiles
Meat eaters

Their eyes are high on their heads so that they can see while they are in the water.

Bb

Beavers

Mammals
Plant eaters

Beavers' teeth grow, like our hair. They have to nibble on trees to keep their teeth from getting too long!

Cc

Cheetahs

Mammals
Meat eaters

Cheetahs usually run about 30 miles per hour (mph) but can run short distances at 60 or 70 mph!

Dd

Dolphins

Mammals
Meat eaters

Even though dolphins live in the ocean, they breathe air.

Ee

Elephants

Mammals
Plant eaters

Elephants can use their trunks to pick berries or to push over trees.

Ff

Frogs

Amphibians
Meat eaters

There are over 4,900 species of frogs in the world that range in size from ½ inch to 15 inches.

Gg

Gorillas

Mammals
Plant eaters

Their hands are similar to ours—five fingers, and they even have "thumbs."

Hh

Hippopotamus

Mammals
Plant eaters

They can close their nostrils so they don't get water up their noses!

Ii

Iguanas

Reptiles
Plant eaters

Iguanas are lizards that live all over the world including rainforests and deserts.

Jj

Jackrabbits

Mammals
Plant eaters

Jackrabbits have very long ears – up to five inches long.

Kk

Koalas

Mammals
Plant eaters

Koalas have extra fur on their bottoms to keep them comfortable while sitting in trees.

Ll

Lions

Mammals
Meat eaters

Lions sleep between 16 and 20 hours a day.

Mm

Manatees

Mammals
Plant eaters

Manatees sometimes use their front flippers to push food into their mouths.

Nn

Newts

Amphibians
Meat eaters

Newts have four "toes" on their front feet and five "toes" on their back feet.

Oo

Owls

Birds
Meat eaters

Their eyes are very big in order to let the light in at night.

Pp

Penguins

Birds
Meat eaters

These birds do not fly, but they swim and can see underwater.

Qq

Quails

Birds
Plant eaters

Quails "marry" for life.

Rr

Rhinoceroses

Mammals
Plant eaters

Men hunt Rhinos for their horns, and these mammals are close to extinction.

Ss

Sea Lions

Mammals
Meat eaters

Sea lions can dive up to 600 feet in order to get their fish dinner.

Tt

Tigers

Mammals
Meat eaters

After eating, tigers bury leftovers in order to hide them from other animals.

Uu

Urials

Mammals
Plant eaters

Urials are a type of wild sheep that live high in the mountains.

Vv

Vultures

Birds
Meat eaters

Vultures' heads don't have many feathers so they won't get all dirty when they eat.

Ww

Wolves

Mammals
Meat eaters

Wolves hunt as a group but will only kill animals that they will eat.

Xx

X-ray Fish

Fish
Meat eaters

These tiny fish (less than two inches long) live in some freshwater rivers in South America.

Yy

Yak

Mammals
Plant eaters

Himalayan Natives use yaks to carry things high in the mountains.

Zz

Zebra

Mammals
Plant eaters

Zebras can be identified by their stripe patterns.